The Mystery of the Wedding Cake

THREE COUSINS DETECTIVE CLUB®

The Mystery of the Wedding Cake

Elspeth Campbell Murphy
Illustrated by Joe Nordstrom

BETHANY HOUSE PUBLISHERS
MINNEAPOLIS, MINNESOTA 55438

THE MYSTERY OF THE WEDDING CAKE
Copyright © 1998
Elspeth Campbell Murphy

Cover and story illustrations by Joe Nordstrom
Cover design by Sheryl Thornberg

THREE COUSINS DETECTIVE CLUB® and TCDC® are
registered trademarks of Elspeth Campbell Murphy.

Scripture quotations are from the *International Children's Bible, New
Century Version,* copyright © 1986, 1988 by Word Publishing,
Dallas, Texas 75039. Used by permission.

Published by Bethany House Publishers
A Ministry of Bethany Fellowship International
11300 Hampshire Avenue South
Minneapolis, Minnesota 55438

Printed in the United States of America by
Bethany Press International, Minneapolis, Minnesota 55438

Library of Congress Cataloging-in-Publication Data

Murphy, Elspeth Campbell.
    The mystery of the wedding cake / by Elspeth Campbell Murphy.
        p. cm. — (Three Cousins Detective Club ; 19)
    Summary: While attending a fancy wedding, the three detective
cousins investigate the mysterious disappearance of the wedding cake.
    ISBN 1–55661–857–3 (pbk.)
    [1. Weddings—Fiction. 2. Cousins—Fiction. 3. Mystery and
detective stories.] I. Title. II. Series: Murphy, Elspeth
Campbell. Three Cousins Detective Club ; 19.
[Fic]—dc21   97–455440
                                                     CIP
                                                        AC

ELSPETH CAMPBELL MURPHY has been a familiar name in Christian publishing for over fifteen years, with more than seventy-five books to her credit and sales reaching five million worldwide. She is the author of the best-selling series *David and I Talk to God* and *The Kids From Apple Street Church*, as well as the 1990 Gold Medallion winner *Do You See Me, God?* A graduate of Trinity College and Moody Bible Institute, Elspeth and her husband, Mike, make their home in Chicago, where she writes full time.

Contents

"Anger is cruel. It destroys like a flood. But who can put up with jealousy!"

Proverbs 27:4

1

The Junior Bridesmaid

"*F*or the last time," said Sarah-Jane Cooper through clenched teeth. "I am not the flower girl. I am the junior bridesmaid. And if you don't know the difference, I feel sorry for you."

Her cousins Timothy Dawson and Titus McKay looked at each other and grinned.

"Is everything all right back there?" asked Sarah-Jane's mother, turning around from the front seat of the car.

"It would be fine," replied Sarah-Jane, "if two certain people I could name knew the first thing about weddings. Which they obviously *don't!*"

"Are you guys giving my Sarah-Jane a hard time?" asked their aunt.

Timothy and Titus looked around to see

which guys she was talking to.

"Yes, they are," said Sarah-Jane. "And it's very unfair. Because they don't have any responsibilities, and I *do*. I have to walk down the aisle all by myself. All they have to do is sit quietly during the ceremony and not eat like pigs at the reception."

Timothy sighed. "It's terrible what a person has to sit through just to get a piece of cake."

"Yes," said Titus. "But the cake is the best part of the whole wedding."

Sarah-Jane chose not to dignify these remarks with an answer. Instead, she sat back and smoothed her dress. It was her first long, formal dress, and she loved it madly.

It was as if by smoothing down her dress she could also smooth out her feelings. They were pretty mixed up.

In the first place, she was happy—make that *thrilled*—that the bride had asked her to be the junior bridesmaid.

But Sarah-Jane also felt a little shy. That was because she hardly knew the bride, Cindy. Sarah-Jane was related to the groom, Mitch. Mitch was her grown-up boy cousin on her father's side. (Timothy and Titus were her boy cousins on her mother's side.)

So Sarah-Jane was feeling happy and shy. And nervous. Mostly she was nervous because she had missed the rehearsal last night.

She and Timothy and Titus and her parents had been on a working vacation up north at Misty Pines Campground. Something very unusual had happened there. And the cousins, who had a detective club, had solved another mystery. But that meant they were delayed getting back.

When Mitch and Cindy learned that it was going to be hard to get Timothy and Titus home and make it to the church on time, they very nicely invited them to come along.

So there had been a bit of a scramble right after lunch—getting Sarah-Jane into her gown and finding clean shirts for the boys. But they had made it. And they would even get to the church early—with plenty of time for Sarah-Jane to practice.

So just relax, she told herself.

What could possibly go wrong?

2

The Groom

*A*s soon as they pulled into the parking lot, a frantic-looking Mitch rushed over to them. Apparently something had gone wrong.

"Uncle Art! Aunt Sue! I'm so glad you're here! I need to talk to Sarah-Jane!"

Sarah-Jane did not like the sound of this.

Mitch took a deep breath. "See, Sarah-Jane. Sweetheart. Cindy and I need you to do us this big favor. We know you're the junior bridesmaid. And, of course, you should be walking down the aisle by yourself. But the thing is—we need you to walk at the back of the line with the flower girl. Could you do that for us? *Please?*"

Sarah-Jane gulped. "But, Mitch! If I walk

with the flower girl, everyone will think *I'm* a
flower girl, too!"

"No, no!" cried Mitch. "Not at all! You're
very grown-up looking. And you're so smart.
And so dependable—"

Sarah-Jane narrowed her eyes and glared at
him. She wasn't a detective for nothing.
"What's wrong with this kid?" she asked.
"What happened at the rehearsal?"

Now it was Mitch's turn to gulp.

"Well, the flower girl's job is to carry a little
basket of rose petals and scatter them gently in

front of the bride. Right? So last night we had a basket of paper scraps for her to practice with.

"But she—well, she *grabbed* the paper petals by the *fistful*. And . . . and . . . she *hurled* them at the pews, yelling, 'TAKE THAT! AND THAT!' Did I mention that she's rather loud?"

Sarah-Jane's parents and cousins were shaking with laughter.

By this time Mitch was wringing his hands. "Her father is the best man. He can't really watch her because the best man has so much to do. And he has to be up front with me. To make matters worse, her mother is sick and can't be here today. Her grandmother will ride herd—I mean, look after her at the reception.

"So—Sarah-Jane—if you could just get her down the aisle? Maybe show her how to scatter the petals? Maybe grab the basket if she tries to hit anyone with it?"

Sarah-Jane sighed. "OK, Mitch. I'll do my best. But I can't promise anything, you know."

"Oh, thank you! Thank you!" cried Mitch. "I just know everything's going to be perfect! I'm completely calm!"

"So everything else is going OK?" asked Sarah-Jane's mother.

"Oh, perfect! Perfect!" cried Mitch. "Couldn't be better. We're having the reception here in the church hall—with a lovely buffet. The best caterer in town. The man is a genius, Cindy says.

"And Cindy was able to get the best pastry chef to do the cake. He's a genius, too, Cindy says."

"*Two* geniuses!" exclaimed Sarah-Jane's father, laughing.

"Yes!" said Mitch. "The only thing that wasn't working out was the flower girl. And Cindy and I—well, we panicked just a little bit. She's a darling child! But a four-year-old can really mess up a wedding. Then Sarah-Jane came to our rescue! And now we can be *completely calm*!"

Mitch started to hurry off. Then he turned as he thought of something else.

"And do you know what the best part of all this is? You two girls are going to look *so pretty* walking together! It's the funniest thing! You look enough alike to be sisters. You both have exactly the same shade of beautiful red hair.

Just the color of a new penny!"

Timothy, Titus, and Sarah-Jane looked at one another in horror.

It couldn't be—!

3

The Flower Girl

*J*ust then a car pulled into the parking lot. Inside were an older lady and a little girl.

The car had barely stopped moving before the door opened and the flower girl stepped out.

She was dressed in a ruffled white dress with a wreath of flowers in her hair. She looked so delicate and pretty, it was as if a butterfly had somehow changed itself into a little girl.

The butterfly looked over at the cousins, and her eyes opened wide with amazement.

She turned to the lady, who was just getting out of the car, and said, "HEY, NONNIE! LOOK! IT'S *THOSE* GUYS! IT'S *THOSE* GUYS! HEY, YOU GUYS!"

Timothy, Titus, and Sarah-Jane smiled

bravely. "Hey, Patience."

Mitch stared at the cousins as if they had pulled seven-layer wedding cakes out of their ears.

"You *know* her?" he asked.

"*Know* her?" replied Titus.

"We're *related* to her," said Timothy.

"*How?*" gasped Mitch.

"We're *third cousins* with her," explained Sarah-Jane. "Her grandmother and our grandmother are *first cousins*. When we were staying with our grandparents this summer, Patience and her grandmother came to visit for the day."

Sarah-Jane didn't go into any of the details of their visit with Patience. She didn't think it would set Mitch's mind at rest.

"So *this* is Patience!" exclaimed Sarah-Jane's mother, who had heard some of the stories. "Mitch! Do you realize what this means? *Your* best man is *my* second cousin!!"

Then—before anyone could even say "Small world!"—the butterfly bounded toward them, kicking up a ton of gravel in the parking lot.

4

The Relatives

"NO! NO! NO! NO! NO!" cried the butterfly. "You said it wrong! You guys are supposed to call me PENNY! Remember?"

"Why is that?" asked Sarah-Jane's mother before Sarah-Jane could stop her.

It was too late. Patience was off on one of her tall tales.

"It's because one time I had this piggy bank. And it got all fulled up with pennies. And it got bigger and *bigger* until one day— BOOM!—it bursted. And then—and then you know what? The pennies went allllll over. And my *whole house* got fulled up with pennies!"

"Is that true?" asked Sarah-Jane's mother, laughing.

Patience nodded solemnly, while Timothy,

Titus, and Sarah-Jane stood behind her, shaking their heads as hard as they could.

Sarah-Jane said, "There *is* a story about why we call her Penny. But—believe me—that's not it."

Sarah-Jane's mother was still laughing. "Oh, honey! Patience reminds me so much of you when you were that age."

Sarah-Jane put her hands on her hips and opened her mouth to protest. But before she could say anything, Nonnie caught up with Patience.

Everybody said how wonderful it was to see everybody and what was everyone doing here and what a small world it was.

While she was talking, Nonnie knelt down and wiped the little girl's shoes with a tissue. Patience's father was coming in another car, and Sarah-Jane thought Nonnie looked a little frazzled. Patience would do that to you.

"All right, now, young lady," said her grandmother. "You stay off the gravel. We don't want your shoes getting all scuffed and dusty. And stay off the lawn. We don't want grass stains on your dress."

"Then where *can* I go?" asked Patience.

Sarah-Jane didn't think this was an unreasonable question.

"Just stay on the sidewalk with Nonnie. There's a good girl."

Standing on the sidewalk with grown-ups didn't seem to appeal to Patience. She looked around for something better. And she saw it.

"BUT, NONNIE! I want to be with *those* guys. Make them be with me. Pleeeease!"

"Oh, sweetie! Of *course* you can!" cried Sarah-Jane's mother before Sarah-Jane could stop her. "Sarah-Jane, take Patience into the church and start practicing with her. Timothy and Titus, you go, too."

"SARAH-JANE! YOUR MOMMY SAID YOU HAVE TO PRACTICE ME!"

"I know," said Sarah-Jane. "I'm standing right here. I heard her."

She took Patience by the hand and led her toward the church. It was going to be a long day.

5

The Flowers

*T*he bouquets had been delivered and were lined up on a table in the lobby. Just waiting for the wedding. Sarah-Jane felt a little shiver of excitement. She knew the smallest bouquet must be hers. It was sitting next to a little basket of rose petals.

"Oooo!" cried Patience. "I want my Easter basket!"

"It's not an Easter basket," said Titus.

"How do *you* know?" asked Patience.

"Because it just *isn't*," said Timothy.

"*Why* isn't it?" demanded Patience.

She made a grab for the basket, but Sarah-Jane got there first and moved it out of the way. It was time for a little talk.

"Now, Patience—Penny—listen to me.

This is a very special day for Mitch and Cindy. And we don't want to mess it up for them." She looked hard at Patience. "Do we?"

Patience shook her head.

"Good!" said Sarah-Jane. "Now, let's practice, and if you do a good job, then we'll—um—we'll—"

Too late Sarah-Jane realized that she didn't have anything to bargain with.

Timothy came to her rescue. "We'll tiptoe down to the church hall and get a sneak peek at the wedding cake."

Patience seemed to like the idea of doing something that at least sounded sneaky. So she agreed to leave her basket where it was.

"We'll use pretend petals for now," Sarah-Jane said as they walked together slowly down the aisle.

"Why?" asked Patience, obediently scattering pretend petals.

"Because we don't want the real ones getting all crushed before the bride walks on them," explained Sarah-Jane.

"Why?"

"Because the bride is special."

"Why?"

"Aurrggh!" cried Sarah-Jane. "Just don't mess with the basket, OK?"

"OK."

They practiced a couple of more times, and Patience really seemed to be getting the hang of it. Plus, she was really behaving herself. But Sarah-Jane didn't want to push her luck. She figured this would be a good time to go take a look at the wedding cake.

6

The Cake

T he cake was gorgeous.

It stood on a wheeled cart in the church hall, ready to be moved to a place of honor on the buffet table.

From the kitchen came the clink of dishes. But no one was around except for a young man, who was smiling proudly at the cake.

"Did you make that?" Sarah-Jane asked him. She kept her voice low, because she wasn't absolutely sure it was OK to be in there.

The young man grinned. "Are you kidding? I'm just Sam the delivery boy. My boss made this. Chef Rudolpho. He's a genius!"

Sarah-Jane glanced toward the kitchen.

"Chef Frederick," said Sam with a little snort.

Sarah-Jane looked at him in surprise. "Cindy says he's a genius, too."

"Oh, with finger sandwiches maybe," said Sam. "But at a wedding reception, the *cake* is *always* the center of attention. And no one makes better cakes than Chef Rudolpho!"

"It's so cool," breathed Sarah-Jane.

"EX-cellent!" murmured Titus.

"Neat-O!" agreed Timothy.

"What color is it on the inside?" asked Patience.

"Chocolate," said Sam, understanding what she meant. "And the frosting is butter-cream."

This was more than they could stand.

Sarah-Jane hustled herself and her cousins out of the social hall before they did something drastic—like diving headlong into the cake.

It was a funny thing about churches, Sarah-Jane thought. They were all different. And yet they were all sort of the same. She had never been in Cindy's church before. But it reminded her of her own.

There was the social hall and the kitchen. A couple of locked doors—probably leading to the furnace room or the supply closet. At the end of the hallway, she guessed they would find the washrooms. . . .

As if reading her mind, Patience said, "I HAVE TO GO POTTY!"

"We'll meet you back upstairs," said Timothy and Titus, making a break for it.

With a sigh, Sarah-Jane took Patience by the hand and led her down the hall to the ladies' room.

While she was helping Patience wash her hands—without getting either of their dresses wet!—a couple of bridesmaids came in.

They oohed and ahhed over Patience and Sarah-Jane and said a thousand times how pretty they looked together.

By this time, Patience was getting squirmy, and she didn't want to wait for Sarah-Jane.

"What's your hurry?" Sarah-Jane asked her.

Patience sighed as if the answer was obvious. "I have to go tell Nonnie how cute I am!"

Sarah-Jane couldn't help laughing. "OK. Go straight outside to Nonnie, and I'll catch up with you in a few minutes."

She was a little nervous about letting Patience go off by herself. But what trouble

could she possibly get into between the ladies'
room and the sidewalk?

Sarah-Jane got to chatting with the bridesmaids, so it was more than a few minutes
before she got back upstairs.

When she got back, she found Patience sitting quietly on the last pew. But she was under
guard with Timothy and Titus plunked down
sternly on either side of her.

"You'll never guess what we caught her
doing," said Timothy.

7

The Penguin

Sarah-Jane groaned and sank down beside them.

"She was hiding under that table in the lobby," said Titus.

"I was not hiding!" cried Patience indignantly.

"Well, what do *you* call it?" asked Titus.

"I was just being there," said Patience.

"Stand up and turn around," Sarah-Jane said to her. "Let me see your dress."

Patience did as she was told.

The dress had gotten a little wrinkled, but Sarah-Jane didn't think it would be too noticeable. Fortunately, the floor had recently been cleaned. So the dress had just picked up a little bit of dust. Sarah-Jane gave it a little whack, and it came right off.

She was just about to settle back when Timothy said, "And that's not all."

Sarah-Jane sat up straight and stared at him. "There's *more*?"

"Oh, yes," said Titus. "There's more."

Timothy said, "We caught her digging the rose petals out of her basket and putting them in a little pile on the floor."

Patience nodded wisely. "I was very careful, Sarah-Jane. We don't want the petals getting all crushed. That's because the *bride* is the one who's supposed to specially squash them. Right?"

"Patience!" yelped Sarah-Jane. "Why were you messing with the basket at all? I specifically told you not to!"

For a moment Sarah-Jane wondered if this was what it felt like to be somebody's mother.

"I know," said Patience earnestly. "But I had a good reason, Sarah-Jane."

"*What* reason?" cried Sarah-Jane. "What *possible* reason?"

Patience sighed as if she simply couldn't understand what all the fuss was about.

"I *had* to look in my Easter basket," she said. "Because the penguin hided a surprise in it for me. I seed it with my own two eyes before the penguin runned away. But *these* guys—" She pointed an accusing finger at Timothy and Titus. "They came and stopped me. So I didn't get to see my present. I don't like them. They're too strict."

Timothy and Titus burst out laughing.

"Can you *believe* this kid?!" said Timothy.

"It's the tallest tale yet!" said Titus.

But Sarah-Jane looked at Patience's furious little face and said, "You know what's funny?"

"Funny ha-ha? Or funny weird?" asked Timothy.

"Funny weird."

"What's funny weird?" asked Titus.

Sarah-Jane shook her head as if she were surprised herself at what she was saying. "I don't know. This doesn't sound like a tall tale to me. I think in her own strange little way, Patience is telling us the truth."

8

The Tuxedo

"*A penguin?!*" cried Timothy. "Oh, puh-*leeze!*"

Patience sighed and rolled her eyes. "Not a *real* penguin, silly! Whoever heard of a real penguin at a wedding? Puh-*leeze!* It was just someone dressed up like a penguin."

"Someone dressed up like a penguin," repeated Titus. "Oh, well. That explains it."

"No, wait," said Sarah-Jane. "Maybe it *does!*" She turned to Patience. "When you said you saw someone dressed up like a penguin, you didn't mean a costume. You didn't mean someone looked like a giant bird. Did you?"

Patience shook her head wildly.

Sarah-Jane went on. "Do you mean you saw someone dressed up in fancy clothes?"

Patience nodded. "That one."

"OK!" exclaimed Sarah-Jane. "Now we're getting somewhere!"

"Getting *where*?" asked Timothy.

"All I'm saying," replied Sarah-Jane, "is that there's probably a logical explanation for what Patience is telling us. Maybe she saw someone in a tuxedo or something. She didn't know the word *tuxedo*. So she said what it *looked* like to her.

"And she's right. A person in a tuxedo *does* look a little bit like a penguin.

"Or you could turn it around: Penguins look a little bit like they're wearing tuxedos."

"OK," said Titus. "I'll grant you that your tuxedo explanation makes sense. But there's just one little problem: What would some guy from the wedding be doing with the flower girl's basket?"

"Well, there is one other little problem," admitted Sarah-Jane. "I know about these things. This is a semi-formal afternoon wedding. The men aren't wearing tuxedos." She said to Patience, "So I guess it wasn't one of the men from the wedding you saw, was it?"

"No," agreed Patience. Then she added, "It was a lady penguin."

9

The Rose Petals

*F*rom their raised eyebrows, Sarah-Jane could guess what Timothy and Titus were thinking. So she said it before they could.

"OK. OK. So the tuxedo explanation doesn't make sense. None of this makes sense. Maybe it *was* just another tall tale. I thought there was a mystery to solve."

Patience raised her hand as if she were sitting in the Story Circle at her preschool. "Sarah-Jane, I know how to solve the mystery. Just look in the basket."

Timothy, Titus, and Sarah-Jane looked at one another. This was not the first time four-year-old Patience had helped the three great detectives solve a mystery. It was getting embarrassing.

But Patience was right. They had to look in the basket.

The trick was doing it.

While they had been arguing about penguins, the church had begun filling up with people. The air was prickly with excitement. Any minute now, the grown-ups would come to put Patience and Sarah-Jane in line.

They had to act fast.

"Wait here," Sarah-Jane whispered.

Quickly, but very casually, she went out to the table in the lobby and picked up her bouquet. Nothing suspicious about that. She was the junior bridesmaid, after all.

Very casually she picked up the flower girl's basket. Nothing suspicious about that, either. She was just helping out, that's all.

Very, very casually she slipped into the back pew.

"Human shield!" she whispered urgently to Timothy and Titus.

The boys understood immediately what she meant. Patience looked puzzled, but she copied Timothy and Titus.

The boys got up to stretch. At least that's what it would seem like to anyone who happened to be looking. What they were *really* doing was blocking Sarah-Jane from view.

Sarah-Jane grabbed a wedding program, which shook in her hands. *Oh, great,* she thought. *As if I weren't nervous enough, I have to be doing this.* She spread the program open on the pew and held the basket over it. Then, in one swift movement, she turned the basket upside down.

Patience gasped as if she had never seen such badness—even though it had been her idea.

"Shhh!!" said Sarah-Jane.

She lifted the basket away.

They all gasped.

10

The Surprise

"Oh, look," said Patience. "A little key." She sounded both surprised and disappointed. What good was a treat in your Easter basket if it wasn't something to eat or play with?

But she was right. Sitting on top of the little pile of rose petals was a key. Attached to the key was a plain round tag with the initials *F.R.*

Timothy, Titus, and Sarah-Jane stared at the key in disbelief. They hadn't really, truly expected to find anything in the basket at all.

But there was the key.

Whose was it?

What was it doing there?

But suddenly Sarah-Jane thought of something else.

The petals!

She snatched up the key and shoved it into the pocket of her long skirt.

(Sarah-Jane's mother had made her dress. The pattern didn't have pockets. But Mrs. Cooper knew that Sarah-Jane couldn't bear to be without pockets, so she had added them. Sarah-Jane was so glad now that she had!)

Once the key was safely tucked away, Sarah-Jane grabbed another program and set the basket on it right side up.

Then, using the first program as a kind of funnel, she poured the petals back into the basket.

If she thought her hands were shaking before—! Timothy, Titus, and Patience quickly gathered up the stray petals and placed them in the basket.

Sarah-Jane sank back on the pew with a sigh of relief.

"Good as new," Titus reassured her.

Sarah-Jane nodded. No one ever had to know.

And they were not a moment too soon.

Because just then Nonnie and Sarah-Jane's

mother came to get them.

"Nonnie," said Patience. "Sarah-Jane turned my Easter basket upside down and dumped all the petals out."

11

The Bride

Nonnie and Sarah-Jane's mother burst out laughing.

"Patience!" said Nonnie, trying to sound stern. "You know perfectly well that Sarah-Jane did no such thing. You mustn't make up stories about people."

"No, no," said Patience, trying to explain. "It was OK because the penguin made her do it."

"Um-hmmm," said Nonnie. "Turn around. Let me see your dress. Nice and clean! That's good. Now show Nonnie your shoes, there's a good girl."

Sarah-Jane opened her mouth to "fess up" about the rose petals. But it was too late. At that moment, the maid of honor came to get them. It was time for Sarah-Jane and Patience to get in line.

Mrs. Cooper and Nonnie hustled Timothy and Titus off to the pew where Sarah-Jane's father was saving their places.

There was no time for the detective cousins to talk things over.

This was it.

The wedding was about to begin.

Sarah-Jane took Patience by the hand and led her to the back of the line where the bride and her father were waiting.

Cindy looked so beautiful in her long white gown that Sarah-Jane forgot about everything else. Especially when Cindy pulled Sarah-Jane aside, knelt down, and whispered in her ear. It was like getting special attention from a princess.

Cindy said, "Thank you so much for looking after Patience for us. We really appreciate it. She's behaving so beautifully for you!"

Sarah-Jane nodded. "Not to sound conceited or anything—but I think Patience likes to hang around with us. She doesn't want to blow it."

Cindy laughed. "My feelings exactly! This

is the most important day of my life, and I don't want to blow it. But everything is going so perfectly. What can possibly go wrong now? As Mitch would say, 'I'm completely calm!' "

There was something Sarah-Jane wanted to ask Cindy, but for the life of her she couldn't remember what it was.

"What was the secret that bride told you?" demanded Patience when Sarah-Jane got back in line.

Sarah-Jane whispered the secret to Patience—at least part of it. "Cindy said you're doing a beautiful job as the flower girl."

Patience nodded. "Got *that* right!"

Suddenly the background music stopped.

There was a breathless pause.

New music began.

It was time to walk down the aisle.

12

The Ceremony

Once Sarah-Jane's turn came, her nervousness disappeared.

The guests oohed and ahhed at the sight of the shy, delicate little flower girl gently scattering her rose petals.

Ha! thought Sarah-Jane, smiling down on Patience. *If you people only knew!*

But Sarah-Jane was also a great believer in giving credit where credit was due. Patience was doing a wonderful job. You had to hand it to her. They made it all the way down the aisle without a single mishap. Good old Patience.

Sarah-Jane was feeling so relaxed by the time they reached the front of the church that she suddenly remembered what she wanted to ask Cindy.

It was very important.

But Sarah-Jane had been taught that it was impolite to interrupt when people were talking. So—interrupting when people were saying their wedding vows would be really, really, *really* impolite.

Her question would have to wait.

Sarah-Jane slipped her hand into her pocket and felt the mysterious key.

Her question was: Which person at the wedding had the initials F.R.?

Of course, knowing who F.R. was still wouldn't explain how his—or her—key had ended up in the flower girl's basket.

Had someone put it there as some sort of goofy practical joke? Who? Why?

And how were they going to get the key back to F.R. if they couldn't find out who F.R. was?

Sarah-Jane wished she could talk this over with Timothy and Titus!

And one other thing seemed strange to her.

When grown-ups were rushing around, they always said, "Where are my keys? Where are my keys?" They didn't say, "Where is my key?"

So why was there only one key on F.R.'s ring?

There was one person who knew what was going on.

After the ceremony, as they were walking back up the aisle, Sarah-Jane scanned the guests without being too obvious about it. She wanted to see if anyone looked even a little bit like a penguin.

No one did.

13

The Best Man

*A*s junior bridesmaid, Sarah-Jane was one of the wedding people who stood in line to greet the guests. Standing in the receiving line was not something the flower girl had to do. No one expected little flower girls to be able to stand still that long.

So Patience went off with her daddy, the best man, to make sure that everything was in order for the reception.

It wasn't long before Tom North was back. He came up to Mitch and said, "I just need to borrow Sarah-Jane for a minute."

Sarah-Jane looked in surprise from one man to the other. It was an unusual situation. Tom, the best man, was her second cousin once removed on her mother's side. Mitch, the groom, was her first cousin on her father's side.

And it seemed that neither one could get along without her today.

Sarah-Jane and Tom had never met. As she slipped out of line, he shook her hand and thanked her for taking care of Patience.

Sarah-Jane wondered if that's what Tom wanted now—to have her watch Patience some more.

But Patience seemed fine. She and Nonnie were talking with some ladies, who kept telling Patience how cute she was. They looked a little surprised when Patience replied, "GOT *THAT* RIGHT!"

So what was up?

Timothy and Titus must have wondered the same thing, because they came hurrying over. Sarah-Jane quickly introduced them.

Tom said, "I'm glad you're all here. I need you to do a reality check for me. See—we have this 'situation,' and Patience was telling me . . . Well, you know how she is. . . ."

Sarah-Jane nodded wisely. "This is about the penguin, isn't it?"

But Tom just looked at her in confusion.

"Penguin? What penguin? I don't know anything about a penguin. This is about the wedding cake."

By this time they had arrived in the social hall. The buffet table was ready and waiting. It was beautiful. It was full.

But something was missing.

"Where's the cake?" asked Timothy.

Tom took a deep breath. "See, that's what I need to know. Are you asking that because there *ought* to be a cake and it's not here? Or because you actually *saw* a cake and it's not here?"

The cousins stared at him, trying to take this in.

Tom went on, "See, I came to check on things, and I realized that there was no cake. I don't want to alarm Cindy and Mitch until I figure out what's going on. I asked the guy in the kitchen, but he was pretty huffy about it. He said he wasn't asked to make the cake. He never saw it delivered. And it wasn't his responsibility."

Tom paused and took another deep breath. "So I was just about to call the bakery and read them the riot act. But Patience said the cake *was* delivered—by a boy named Sam. But she also said it reached all the way to the ceiling and that Rudolph the Red-Nosed Reindeer made it. She said you guys saw it, too. *Did* you see the cake?"

"Yes, we did," said Timothy.

"The delivery boy's name was Sam," said Titus. "The cake did *not* touch the ceiling—but maybe it looked that way to Patience, looking up at it. As far as Rudolph, I have no idea . . ."

"Chef Rudolpho," said Sarah-Jane. "Chef Rudolpho made the cake."

"OK!" said Tom. "We've got that all figured out. There really was a cake. The question is—where is it now?"

14

The T.C.D.C.

*T*he cousins looked at one another.

A missing wedding cake?

This was a disaster!

The wedding ceremony had gone beautifully. Patience had not messed up at all. Mitch and Cindy were happily married.

But there was still the reception. And Sarah-Jane knew that Mitch and Cindy would see a missing wedding cake as . . . well, as a disaster.

"I'm not quite sure what to do," said Tom. "Unless someone snuck in here and stole it—which doesn't seem likely—it's got to be around here someplace."

"We'll help you look," said Timothy.

"We're good at that," said Titus.

"You can count on the T.C.D.C.," said Sarah-Jane.

"What's a 'teesy-deesy'?" asked Tom.

"IT'S LETTERS!" said Patience.

No one had heard her come in. They heard her now.

"Capital B. Capital V. Capital P. Capital Z. It stands for the Three Cousins Detective Club," said Patience, looking very pleased with herself. (She had learned about the T.C.D.C. when she met Timothy, Titus, and Sarah-Jane at their grandparents' earlier that summer.)

"Right, Sarah-Jane?"

"Close enough," said Sarah-Jane. "But the T.C.D.C. is busy right now. We'll play with you later, OK?"

"OK, Sarah-Jane. But can I have my surprise back?"

"What surprise?" asked her father.

"The one the penguin hided in my Easter basket, of course!" said Patience.

Tom looked helplessly at Sarah-Jane. "Do you have any idea what she's talking about?" he asked.

"Yes," said Sarah-Jane. An idea was beginning to take shape in her mind. "Yes, I do."

She pulled the key out of her pocket.

Tom blinked at it. "How did you get *that*? There's a whole pegboard of keys like that in the kitchen."

"Oh!" exclaimed Sarah-Jane, more to herself than the others. "F.R. is not a *person*. F.R. is a *place*. A place in the *church*."

"We're not sure how we got it," said Timothy, answering Tom's question. "We think someone hid it in the rose petal basket."

"*Who?*" asked Tom. "*Why?*"

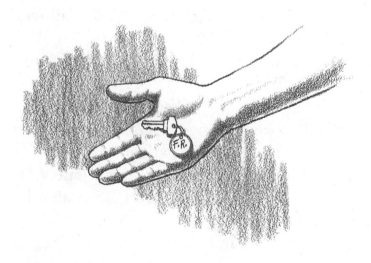

Titus shrugged. "We don't know that, either. And it was a lousy hiding place, when you stop to think about it. Because, when the petals were gone, Patience would have been sure to see the key. And—no offense—she wouldn't be real quiet about it."

Patience sighed as if she didn't know what the problem was. "The lady penguin hided a surprise for me in my Easter basket."

Sarah-Jane said slowly, "The penguin didn't put the key in the basket to *hide* it. She put it where she knew it would be *found*."

"*Penguin?*" said Tom, looking as if he wanted to go lie down. "Who is this penguin you all keep talking about?"

Sarah-Jane shook her head apologetically. "I have no idea. All I know is that she wants us to look in the furnace room."

15

The Penguin Again

"ME! ME! ME! MY TURN! LET *ME* DO IT!"

Rather than argue, Sarah-Jane handed Patience the key. It hadn't fit in the first two locked doors they had tried. Maybe Patience would have better luck.

At first they thought they had the wrong door again. But Patience got the key to fit. She turned the key in the lock and opened the door.

"Oh, look!" she exclaimed. "A great big cake. And I finded it!"

"Yes, you did," said Sarah-Jane. "You most certainly did."

The wedding cake was fine.

Tom carefully pulled out the cart and

wheeled it across the room. There was no space for it on the buffet table. But it got even more attention standing by itself.

"I don't understand any of this," muttered Tom. "Is this someone's idea of a joke?"

"I don't think so," said Sarah-Jane. "But I don't understand it, either."

Just then the rest of the bridal party and the guests came in.

"Oh, Mitch!" cried Cindy happily. "Just look at the cake! Isn't it lovely?"

"Just perfect," agreed Mitch.

Tom and the cousins exchanged an understanding glance. There was no need to tell Mitch and Cindy how close they had come to having no cake at all. At least not now.

Patience said, "Rudolph the Red-Nosed Reindeer made that cake. And then the penguin hided it in the closet. But I finded it."

Everyone laughed delightedly.

"Isn't she darling?" someone exclaimed.

"And such an imagination!" said someone else.

"Come on," said Sarah-Jane to Patience and the boys. "We need to put this key back in the kitchen."

She wanted to get Patience out of there before she said any more charming things.

They were a little afraid of running into the grumpy Chef Frederick. But when they stepped into the kitchen, all they saw was one flustered young woman. She looked like she was about to cry. She was wearing a kind of waiter's uniform. Black pants. Black jacket. Crisp white shirt. Red bow tie.

"Oh, look!" said Patience. "The lady penguin."

The young woman hadn't heard them come in. She was so startled she almost dropped a tray.

"We brought your key back," said Sarah-Jane.

"What? Mine? No, that's not—! How? How did you know?"

"Patience saw you hide the key," said Sarah-Jane. "Do you want to tell us what's going on?"

The young woman, who said her name was Jan, sank down on a stool.

"I hid the key," said Jan. "But I didn't hide the cake. Chef Frederick did that."

"*Why?*" gasped the cousins.

"Because he was so jealous of Chef Rudolpho's wedding cakes," said Jan. "This was the prettiest cake ever. So Frederick decided to hide the cake. It would look like Rudolpho had messed up and not delivered it. Frederick didn't know you kids had seen it. But I did. So as soon as he hid the cake, I snuck the key and hid it in the basket."

"Why didn't you just tell someone?" asked Titus.

Jan said, "Because I didn't want people to know what Frederick had done. He's a genius. But people aren't going to put up with behavior like that. He wouldn't have gotten more jobs. And I didn't want Frederick to know I had gone behind his back to help you. *I* would have been out of a job."

The cousins looked around nervously.

"Where is Frederick now?" asked Sarah-Jane.

"He left!" wailed Jan. "He saw you find the cake, and he realized I gave you the key. So he left. I'm just the assistant. What am I going to do?"

"Get another boss!" said Titus.

"First thing Monday morning," agreed

Jan. "But that doesn't help me now."

"Not to worry," said Sarah-Jane. "I happen to know two of the nicest ladies in the world. They would be glad to help you. Patience— run get Nonnie and my mother."

It took a while—quite a while—to explain about this latest disaster. But then Nonnie and Mrs. Cooper stepped right in. The reception went off without a hitch.

"You know," Cindy said to the cousins later, "so many things can go wrong at a wedding. But this one was perfect. Absolutely perfect."

Timothy, Titus, and Sarah-Jane looked at one another, uncertain of what to say.

Then, from under the buffet table, came the gentle voice of a butterfly: "GOT *THAT* RIGHT!"

The End

Series for Young Readers*
From Bethany House Publishers

★ ★ ★

THE ADVENTURES OF CALLIE ANN
by Shannon Mason Leppard
Readers will giggle their way through the true-to-life escapades of Callie Ann Davies and her many North Carolina friends.

★ ★ ★

BACKPACK MYSTERIES
by Mary Carpenter Reid
This excitement-filled mystery series follows the mishaps and adventures of Steff and Paulie Larson as they strive to help often-eccentric relatives crack their toughest cases.

★ ★ ★

THE CUL-DE-SAC KIDS
by Beverly Lewis
Each story in this lighthearted series features the hilarious antics and predicaments of nine endearing boys and girls who live on Blossom Hill Lane.

★ ★ ★

RUBY SLIPPERS SCHOOL
by Stacy Towle Morgan
Join the fun as home-schoolers Hope and Annie Brown visit fascinating countries and meet inspiring Christians from around the world!

★ ★ ★

THREE COUSINS DETECTIVE CLUB®
by Elspeth Campbell Murphy
Famous detective cousins Timothy, Titus, and Sarah-Jane learn compelling Scripture-based truths while finding—and solving—intriguing mysteries.

* (ages 7–10)